SUPER HERO
ADVENTURES

Buggin' Out!

With Spider-Man, Ant-Man, the Wasp, and Doctor Octopus

By **MacKenzie Cadenhead**
& Sean Ryan

Illustrated by **Derek Laufman**

MARVEL
Los Angeles
New York

Dedication
For Miles & his pals at the Mount Sinai NICU —MC
For Joanna, always —SR

MarvelHQ.com

© 2018 MARVEL. All rights reserved. Published by Marvel Press, an imprint of Disney Book Group. No part of this book may be reproduced or transmitted in any form or by any means, electronic or mechanical, including photocopying, recording, or by any information storage and retrieval system, without written permission from the publisher. For information address Marvel Press, 125 West End Avenue, New York, New York 10023.

Designed by David Roe
Painted by Anna Beliashova and Vita Efremova

Printed in the United States of America
First Paperback Edition, June 2018
10 9 8 7 6 5 4 3 2
Library of Congress Control Number: 2017955190
ISBN 978-1-368-00857-0
FAC-029261-18271

SUSTAINABLE
FORESTRY
INITIATIVE
Certified Sourcing
www.sfiprogram.org
SFI-01415

Spider-Man

Peter Parker was just a normal kid when he was bitten by a radioactive spider and became **The Amazing Spider-Man**! He has super strength, can climb walls, and can jump incredible distances. Being the science-minded kid that he is, Peter also made his very own web-shooters. Peter takes his job as a Super Hero seriously because of the lesson his Uncle Ben taught him: With great power comes great responsibility.

Ant-Man & the Wasp

Ant-Man and the Wasp prove that big things come in small packages. Thanks to the incredible Pym Particles that can shrink anything, Scott Lang can become the size of an ant while keeping the strength of a full-grown person. With the help of his high-tech suit, he can communicate with colonies of ants to enlist their help with his super heroics. Similarly, the brilliant scientist Hope Van Dyne uses Pym Particles to shrink down. But her suit includes a set of ultralight yet powerful wings and a stinger that gets the job done.

Doctor Octopus

Doctor Octopus wasn't always a vicious villain with four menacing metal tentacles. He was once Dr. Otto Octavius, a supersmart scientist. One fateful day, he was working on his experimental robot arms when a terrible accident fused them to his body. The dastardly doctor has since turned to a life of crime, controlling the metal tentacles with his mind to stir up trouble.

Chapter
1

"Jaeger."

"Bacharach."

"Choi."

"Schulte."

The students whose names were called stood beside their team captains, Missy Ruiz and Flash Thompson.

"I'll take Buck next," Missy said. She gave Buck a high five.

"Powell's with me," said Flash. Powell joined his cheering teammates.

"That leaves Murphy and Parker," Coach Bennett said. He pointed at the two boys standing on the sidelines of the basketball court.

Donnie Murphy looked at his feet. He didn't like basketball. He didn't like sports of any kind. He hoped that if he didn't make eye contact he would never be picked.

Peter Parker, on the other hand, was eager to join a team. While Peter had the reputation of being an uncoordinated brainiac, he secretly loved playing sports. He secretly loved doing anything athletic. Because secretly, he was the arachnid acrobat known as Spider-Man!

In order to keep his Super Hero identity secret, Peter always had to play down his amazing skills. But today he just wanted to participate. Even if he only used ten percent of his ability, Peter knew he could be the star of Midtown High's PE program. And after years of being picked last, he wanted to shine.

Peter smiled at Missy as she considered her choice. *Pick me*, he thought. *Pick me!*

"Murphy," Missy said.

Peter's shoulders slumped.

"I guess Parker's with us," said Flash.

Peter straightened up. He could still show them what he could do! But as he went to join his team, Flash blocked his path.

Flash was the most athletic boy at school. He was big and strong, and though he might not have been at the top of any class other than Gym, Peter was eager to hear his words of wisdom. "Why don't you sit this one out, Parker?" Flash said. "Hold up the wall with Murphy while the rest of us athletes play four-on-four. We'll make sure the ball never comes near you."

This was not the pep talk Peter was hoping for. He opened his mouth to tell Flash that he actually wanted to play. But before he could speak, Peter's spider-sense began to tingle. A basketball was about to hit the back of his head!

Peter's mind raced. What should he do? If he spun around and caught the ball, everyone would see his quick reflexes. Then they'd all want him on their team! But if he caught a ball he clearly couldn't see, his classmates might start to wonder how he did it. And his secret identity as Spider-Man would be compromised.

Could he risk it? No. The only choice was to let the ball hit him. Peter braced for impact.

Suddenly, Flash reached out and caught the ball. "That was a close one," he said. "Like I was saying, stay out of our way, Parker. Wouldn't want that big brain of yours to get hurt."

Flash laughed and joined the rest of the boys and girls on the court. Coach Bennett blew his whistle and started the game. Peter walked over to the sideline where Donnie Murphy had already sat down.

Donnie relaxed against the gymnasium wall. "Lucky we don't have to play, huh?" he said.

Peter watched as Flash tossed the basketball into the net. *SWISH!*

"Yeah." Peter sighed. "Lucky us."

Chapter 2

Despite the morning's basketball bust, Peter's afternoon was looking up. It was time for the school science fair. This year it was being held at Empire State University, and the real scientists who worked there would be the judges. At stake was the coveted Big Apple Science Trophy. Peter knew the competition would be fierce. But he also knew how hard he had worked on his project. He was confident he had a shot at winning the top prize.

"I'd like to see Flash Thompson do
something like this," Peter mumbled to
himself, steaming all over again as he
remembered how Flash had sunk shot
after shot in PE.

"What was that?" asked Aunt May.
She had come all the way from Queens
to see her nephew in scientific action.

"I said, uh, thanks for coming to
this," Peter replied.

"I wouldn't miss it for anything,"
said Aunt May. "Although I must
admit, I don't entirely understand what

your project is about." She pointed to the large tub of water that Peter was wheeling into the science fair room. Inside the tub were four long metal poles connected by wires.

"I call it *A New Kind of Current*," Peter said. "I'm showing how we can create electricity by using water's natural movement. I got the idea after we went to the beach and the waves kept pushing me back out of the water. There's a lot of power in those waves! So for my project I figured out how to take that power and turn it into electrical energy."

Aunt May raised her eyebrows. "All I think about at the beach is who the bad guy is in the Agatha Twisty mystery I'm reading." She squeezed her nephew's arm. "Peter, I am very impressed."

Peter blushed. For a moment all thoughts of Flash Thompson and basketball were forgotten. Until . . .

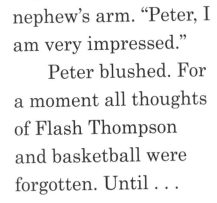

"Excuse me. Coming through!" said Flash. His shirt was untucked and his hair was a mess. The normally cucumber-cool athlete was anything but as he stumbled into the fair room carrying a glass case and some index cards.

Flash dumped his stuff on the table next to Peter's. Peter rolled his eyes. He wondered what on earth Flash Thompson could be presenting at the science fair. How many basketball players it takes to screw in a lightbulb?

"Oh, hey, Parker," Flash said, as he glanced up from his project. "I had to run here from basketball practice. I was worried I'd be late." Flash looked around. Though it was cool in the fair room, he continued to sweat. "Yikes, there's a lot of smart stuff in here."

Peter smiled. "There sure is."

"Wow," said Flash. "I didn't know water could make electricity. Your project looks great!"

"Thanks," Peter said. He looked at the jumble of papers on Flash's table. He knew he was being unkind, but he was still hurt by Flash's rude behavior in gym class that morning. It felt good to be better than Flash at something. Trying not to snicker, Peter asked, "What's your project?"

Flash showed Peter his note cards. To Peter's surprise, they had drawings of different types of ants and captions about their special skills. Inside the glass case was a habitat with hundreds of ants. Peter was impressed.

"I call it *Heavy Lifting: The Ant,*" Flash said. "I like ants, you know? They're, like, superstrong."

Peter couldn't believe it. "It looks like you put a lot of effort into your project," he said.

"I've been working on this for weeks," Flash replied.

As Flash set up his project, Peter returned to his table and pouted. If Peter wasn't welcome to play basketball, then Flash shouldn't be able to do science. Peter thought he'd rather be in a big Super Hero fight than watch Flash beat him at the science fair, too.

Little did he know his wish was about to be granted.

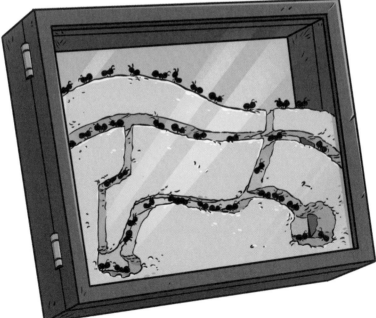

Chapter 3

In another corner of Empire State University, Hope Van Dyne stood before a giant husk of corn in the lab where she and Scott Lang worked. She had encountered enormous vegetables other times when she shrank down to her Super Hero form, the Wasp. But in those cases, the vegetables were normal size, and Hope was super-small. Today was different. Hope was currently regular-human size. And this corn was as big as a minivan.

"It worked!" Hope said. She clapped her hands in excitement. "We've successfully altered the Pym Particles into Gigantor Particles. Usually they allow us to shrink down to insect size, but today we've made them do the opposite—grow organic material bigger! This could be the answer to world hunger. Imagine if we could grow fields of giant corn. Or apples."

"Or pizza!" Scott chimed in. Scott was Hope's partner in the lab—and in battle—as the Super Hero Ant-Man.

"Yes, Scott," Hope said. She rolled her eyes. "Or pizza." She walked over to the particle spectrometer at the far end of their lab. She pulled a canister from its base and made sure the lid was shut tight. "This is just our first test. We still have to make sure the organic compounds maintain their atomic structure when enlarged."

"Which is science talk for big corn same as little corn?" Scott asked.

Hope nodded and tossed him the canister.

"That canister contains the only collection of Gigantor Particles that can enlarge organic matter," she explained. "This is one of the most important scientific breakthroughs in generations. We have to keep it safe. In other words, don't open it."

Scott fastened the canister to the holster of his Ant-Man suit. "You can count on me," he said. "Or my name isn't—"

BOOM!

The door to the lab burst open and a menacing man with four metal tentacles pushed through the doorway.

"Doctor Octopus!" Scott shouted.

A tentacle shot into the room and snatched the canister containing the Gigantor Particles from Ant-Man's suit.

"The one and only," the Super Villain said as an evil grin spread across his face.

Chapter 4

Ant-Man and the Wasp stood opposite the sinister scientist, stunned.

"The Gigantor Particles belong to me now," Doctor Octopus said. "I will use them on myself, and then there will be no stopping me! I will be huge, and the world will be mine to do with as I wish!"

Doc Ock's metal arms flailed around the laboratory. Wasp and Ant-Man jumped out of the way just as one crashed down between them. Ant-Man shrank down to his ant size, while the full-size Wasp flew over to confront the villain.

"The Gigantor Particles are experimental," she said, trying to stay calm. "We don't know how they work on humans yet. You're putting yourself in danger if you open that canister."

"Silly insect," Doc Ock said. "I don't need you to finish this work. I have the superior scientific mind. I will make these particles perform perfectly. And then I will squash you like the bugs you are."

Doc Ock froze. "Wait, there's only one of you? I thought there were two. Where did the other one go? Where is the little ant boy?"

"That's Ant-MAN to you!" a tiny voice said from the tip of a tentacle's pincer. It held the canister of Gigantor Particles. Ant-Man pried the claw open and the canister fell to the ground.

"Noooo!" Doctor Octopus cried. He reached for the plummeting particles, but he was too slow.

"Gotcha," the Wasp said. She'd shrunk down now, too. She caught the canister before it hit the floor. Then she flew out of the laboratory with it.

Ant-Man followed on foot.

Doctor Octopus came right behind him.

The chase was on!

Chapter 5

Three judges stood before Flash's ant project.

"Sometimes even the strongest ant needs some help," Flash said. "Sure, he can lift up to five thousand times his own weight, but when there's something that's too heavy to carry on his own, that little guy will call on his friends to help him out. I tested this by leaving out a superheavy Cheerio, and sure enough a group of five ants worked together to carry it away.

I guess you could say ants have got brains *and* brawn!" The science fair judges laughed. Flash smiled. Peter frowned.

This was really happening. Flash Thompson was doing well at science. And worse, Peter himself was interested in Flash's project. Peter knew he shouldn't be so annoyed. Assuming Flash wouldn't be good at schoolwork just because he was good

at sports was unfair. Just as unfair
as Flash thinking Peter couldn't play
basketball because he was smart. But
Peter didn't care about fairness right
now. He just wanted the judges to stop
paying attention to Flash.

Which they did, the moment
Doctor Octopus came raging through
the door. Panic ensued at the sight of
the metal-tentacled menace.

"Give me those particles!" Doc Ock
cried.

Ant-Man was right beside him. "What's the magic word?" he asked.

Doctor Octopus swung a metal arm.

Ant-Man ducked. "Please," the tiniest Avenger said. "The magic word is *please.*"

"Enough of this foolishness!" said Doctor Octopus. "I am the superior scientist! The altered Pym Particles will be mine. And you will give them to me now!"

Peter was wondering what particles they were talking about when he noticed a lone canister floating through the air. It moved with direction and purpose, as if someone very small was flying it. Suddenly it dipped down and shot past Aidan Taylor's homemade volcano before disappearing into Reilly First's dry-ice project.

Peter knew what he had to do.

As scientists and students scattered, Peter grabbed Aunt May and pushed her out the door to safety. Amid the chaos, he disappeared back into the crowd. Peter hated leaving his aunt, but he needed to help. He needed to find an empty classroom to change. He needed to become *the amazing Spider-Man!*

Chapter 6

Doctor Octopus slammed his tentacles down hard on the floor. Ant-Man weaved between them. He got in close to Doc Ock's body and slammed against his chest with all his might. The mad scientist stumbled backward. Ant-Man was about to land another punch when a metal arm swiped right and knocked him through the air.

Ant-Man landed in the jaws of
a pincer. The menacing metal claw
began to close. Ant-Man was as good as
squashed until . . .

FWOOSH!

The Wasp swooped in. She lifted
Ant-Man out of the tentacle's grasp and
flew him to safety.

"I've really got to get me some
wings," Ant-Man said.

"You're welcome," replied the Wasp.

"RAAARRRR!" roared Doctor
Octopus. He grabbed hold of the nearest
table and flipped it. Science projects
flew everywhere, including Reilly's dry-
ice experiment. The canister of Gigantor
Particles rolled out from the mist.

"The particles!" the Wasp cried.
She dropped Ant-Man at the foot of the
artificial volcano and flew as fast as
she could for the canister.

She reached out a hand.

She almost had it when—
SLAM! One of Doc Ock's
tentacles swatted
her aside.

The evil scientist
lifted the canister.
"Victory," he cried.
"Victory is mine!"

The Wasp called to Ant-Man, "I think it's time we let Doctor Octopus know what Pym Particles actually feel like."

"Roger that," said Ant-Man. He took a gas balloon filled with shrinking Pym Particles from his utility belt and hurled it at the Super Villain.

Just then, Spider-Man swung onto the scene. He had timed his entrance perfectly. The trajectory of his swing was right on track. He knocked Doctor Octopus off his feet and sent them both flying . . . right into Ant-Man's shrinking balloon!

BURST!

Spider-Man, Doctor Octopus, and the canister of Gigantor Particles shrank down to insect size. They tumbled into the Amanat cousins' group project, landing inside the jaws of a Venus flytrap!

Chapter 7

Spider-Man lay on his side, face-to-face with Doctor Octopus. The Venus flytrap began to close.

"I don't know what's worse," Spidey said. "The fact that I'm the size of a lima bean and I'm about to be eaten by a plant, or the fishy breath on *you*." He waved his hand in front of his nose. "Is that why they call you Doctor *Octopus*? Pee-yew!"

"Enough, you bothersome bug!" Doc Ock shoved the web-slinger aside. He spotted the canister of Gigantor Particles caught between two of the flytrap's teeth. His now-tiny metal tentacles lifted him toward it, but before he could reach out, Spider-Man tackled him from behind.

"I don't know what those particles do," Spidey said. "But I'm guessing they're not for you!" He webbed Doc Ock's metal extremities together and hurled him toward the ceiling. The fearsome foe flew up and out of the plant's jaws, taking Spider-Man with him. They crash-landed on top of a table.

"You fool!" Doctor Octopus cried. "The canister will be crushed!"

Ant-Man ran up beside them. "Octopuppy's right," he said. "If those particles are released, there's going to be a giant man-eating plant in the middle of Manhattan."

While Doctor Octopus and Ant-Man stared in horror at the flytrap's closing jaws, Spider-Man stared in awe at his fellow Super Hero. "Excuse me, Ant-Man," he said. "Hi, I'm your friendly neighborhood Spider-Man, and can I just say I love your work with the Avengers? Seriously, this is *huge*. Or should I say *tiny*? You know, because we're small?" He laughed at his own joke. "Anyway, I've always wanted to team up with you. And now you're here, and I'm here, so maybe we can—" Spider-Man paused. "I'm sorry, did

you say 'giant man-eating plant'? The particles make things bigger?"

Ant-Man nodded.

Spidey hung his head. "My bad."

The trio watched as the plant's leaves tightened and the canister was about to burst.

"I can't look," Ant-Man said, turning away.

Suddenly, the Wasp swooped in, grabbed the canister, and saved the day.

She landed beside Ant-Man. He gave her a high five. "I knew we'd be okay!" he exclaimed.

"Enough! The particles will be mine!" Doctor Octopus yelled. His tentacles moved into action, each one knocking a hero aside. The canister flew into the air once more. Doc Ock reached for it, but Spider-Man's web snatched it first.

As he handed the canister to the Wasp, Spider-Man said, "May I just say it's a real honor to be fighting alongside— Oof!"

A tentacle grabbed Spider-Man and hurled him into the air. The Wasp jumped out of the path of another. "Ant-Man," she hollered. "Go long!"

Ant-Man took off, and the Wasp threw the canister. It sailed over Doctor Octopus's head and landed right in Ant-Man's arms.

Ant-Man climbed through a project about climate change (*CO$_2$ Much?*) and ran past a poster on running (*Fartlek Training: It's Not Just a Silly Name!*). But Doc Ock was gaining on him. By the time Ant-Man reached the base of the baking-soda volcano, the brilliant bad guy was on his heels.

"Ant-Man," Spider-Man called from the top of the volcano. "Up here!" But just as Ant-Man launched the canister, the ground began to shake. A low rumbling sound got louder and louder until . . .

KA-BAAAAAM!

The volcano erupted, sending Spider-Man and the canister flying. He shot his web at it.

"Got it! No thanks to that eruption interruption," he said. Spider-Man was so relieved to have the Gigantor Particles in his possession that he didn't notice he had landed—and was stuck—in a petri dish of honey!

"Well, this is a sticky situation," he said.

"Or a sweet one," Doctor Octopus laughed, suddenly upon him. "Good-bye, spider-fool!" he cried as he snatched the canister from Spider-Man's gooey hand and ran.

Chapter 8

Doctor Octopus headed for the exit. If he made it outside before the heroes caught him, he could disappear. Then he—and the Gigantor Particles—would be gone for good!

Spider-Man tried to run forward through the honey, but it was like pushing against the waves at the beach. If only he could use the thickness of the sweet nectar to his advantage, like how he'd harnessed the power of the water's current in his science project.

A lightbulb went off over Spidey's head! He knew exactly what to do.

Ant-Man and the Wasp arrived to pull him free. As they tugged, Spider-Man said, "I know you guys are Avengers and all, but I think I know how to catch Doctor Octopus."

"Tell us your big idea, kid," Ant-Man said.

"Ant-Man, grab that spoon and stick it in the honey," Spider-Man instructed.

Ant-Man shoved the handle of the utensil into the thick amber goop.

"Wasp, can you pull the top part back as far as possible?"

"I sure can," the Wasp replied. She flew to the tip of the spoon, bent it all the way backward, and held it there.

Spider-Man climbed into the bowl of the makeshift catapult and curled himself into a ball. "Here goes nothing," he said. He gave the Wasp a thumbs-up. She let go.

Spider-Man catapulted into the air with such force that it didn't take long for him to reach Doctor Octopus and knock him to the ground. The Super

Villain went sprawling, and the canister fell from his hand. It smashed open. The Gigantor Particles spilled all over them both.

"Oh no!" Spidey cried.

"Oh yes!" Doc Ock replied.

"We're going to be giants," they said in unison.

As the particles took hold, the Super Hero and the Super Villain grew and grew and grew until . . . they were back to their normal size.

"Huh," said Spider-Man. "The giant version of tiny us is regular-size us. That's a lesson in proportion."

"You fool!" cried Doctor Octopus. "You've ruined everything!"

Spider-Man shrugged. "And I'd say I saved the world. We'll just have to agree to disagree."

Doctor Octopus shot a tentacle at Spider-Man, knocking him off his feet. "I don't need to be huge to exterminate you irritating insects!" he cried. "Or to destroy the entire university!" Doctor Octopus began rampaging through the science fair.

Ant-Man and the Wasp returned to their regular size. They helped Spider-Man to his feet.

"We have to stop him," Ant-Man said.

"I've got it," the Wasp cried. She pointed to Flash's science project and the glass case that housed his ants. "All we have to do is break this open and we've got ourselves an army!"

"On it," Ant-Man said. He raised his fist and was about to smash the case when Spider-Man snatched it away.

"I'm sorry," Spidey said. "But I can't let you do that."

Chapter 9

"Oh no," said Ant-Man. "Did Doc Ock do some sort of mind control on you? I hate it when the bad guys do mind control."

"No, it's not that," Spider-Man said. "It's just that this is someone's science fair project and I know he worked really hard on it. I'd feel bad if we destroyed it."

"But Ant-Man can use neurotransmitters from his helmet to communicate with the ants," the Wasp explained. "He can send them into Doctor Octopus's metal arms so they can chew through the wires he uses to control them. The battle would be over in an instant."

"Really?" asked Spider-Man. "Wow, that *is* an awesome plan." He pictured Flash and all the hard work he had done. He shook his head. "But no. We can't."

"Sure you can," said a voice from behind a table. Flash Thompson popped his head out. "Those are my ants. If they can help stop Doctor Octopus, then they're all yours, Spider-Man."

"Are you sure?" Spidey asked. "Your project would be ruined."

Flash shrugged. "It's no biggie. The guy next to me with that awesome water project is probably going to win the trophy anyway. At least now my ants will be doing some good. I knew they were the coolest insects!"

Ant-Man smiled.

"No offense, Spider-Man," Flash said.

"None taken," answered Spidey.

"And listen," Flash added. "If you want to chew through wires, use the trap-jaw ants. Their mandibles move crazy fast, like a hundred and forty miles per hour. They'll get the job done in a snap."

Spider-Man was impressed. "And here I thought a spider bite was intense."

The Wasp cleared her throat. "Can we get back to beating the bad guy?" she asked.

Spidey nodded.

The Wasp smashed a hole into one side of the glass case.

Ant-Man sent a signal to the trap-jaw ants. In seconds they came streaming from the case and swarmed Doctor Octopus's metal arms. Then they disappeared inside the sockets.

"What is this?" Doc Ock laughed. "You think some tiny, insignificant ants are worthy adversaries for me?"

Spider-Man, Ant-Man, and the Wasp waited.

"I'll show you what real might is!" the villain continued. He raised his tentacles and prepared to bring them down on the three heroes. But before he could, there was a spark and some smoke. His metal arms went limp.

"My arms!" Doctor Octopus cried. "What have you done?"

"That's called short-circuiting,"
Ant-Man said. The trap-jaw ants
streamed out of the tentacles and
returned to his side.

"And these are called web-shooters,"
Spider-Man added. He tied the
tentacles together with his webs.

"And this is known as a wasp sting," said the Wasp. She stunned Doctor Octopus with her stinger.

Then he fell at last, defeated, to the ground.

Chapter 10

Officer Stanley snapped the final handcuff shut. It was a special set of eight cuffs linked together by thick chains.

"And we just had this lying around in the squad car?" Officer Ditko asked his partner.

Officer Stanley nodded. "Two cuffs for the hands, two for the feet, and four for the metal arms," she said. She led Doctor Octopus out of the building and put him in the back of their police cruiser.

Spider-Man lowered himself from the ceiling and addressed Officer Ditko. "Just when you think you've seen it all, am I right?" he said.

Officer Ditko did a double take. Then he shook his head and followed his partner outside.

sweet sips

DOWN UNDER WATER ...LTA

Heavy Lifting: THE ANT

Spider-Man swung over to Ant-Man and the Wasp. "I'm sorry I spilled your Gigantor Particles," Spidey said.

"No worries," replied the Wasp. "We figured it out once. We'll do it again. And maybe this time we'll make it Super Villain–proof."

Ant-Man added, "I'm sorry we made you tiny."

"No big deal," said Spider-Man. "It was actually pretty cool to see things from your perspective. I used to think the bigger the better. But I guess not

always. I mean, look at how tough those ants were!"

"Never underestimate the little guy," Ant-Man agreed.

"Or the big guy," the Wasp added. "There's usually more to people than what you see on the surface."

Spider-Man looked over to where Aunt May was helping Flash clean up his broken science fair project. "There sure is," he agreed. Then he said good-bye to his super pals and swung out of sight.

Chapter 11

Despite the destruction caused by Doctor Octopus, the science fair carried on. Soon it was time to announce the winner of the Big Apple Science Trophy. Peter could barely contain his excitement. He stood beside his project, squeezing Aunt May's hand.

"And the trophy goes to . . ." The head judge opened an envelope. "Peter Parker."

The crowd of scientists, students, and their families applauded. Peter hugged his aunt. He walked to the front of the room to claim his prize. "Thank you," he said to the crowd. "This trophy means a lot to me. But if it's okay with the judges, I'd like to share it with someone else."

Peter pointed to Flash Thompson.

"I got to see Flash's ant project before it was destroyed tonight. And I can tell you it was really good. But even more impressive? It was Flash's project that saved the day. I heard that when Spider-Man, Ant-Man, and the Wasp needed Flash's ants to defeat Doctor Octopus, Flash said yes. He even told them which ants to use, which was some quick and smart thinking. For that, he deserves this award as much as I do."

The crowd cheered. Flash joined Peter at the front of the room and shook his hand, a giant smile on his face.

After the ceremony, Flash pulled Peter aside. "Thanks for including me, Parker," he said. "It means a lot that a smart guy like you thinks I did a good job."

Peter looked at his feet. "To tell you the truth," he said, "I didn't expect you

to make such a good project. I thought you were only interested in sports. I'm sorry I judged you, Flash. I promise not to do that again."

Flash considered this. "So does this mean there's more to you than just being a supersmart guy? Have you got some mad basketball skills I don't know about?"

Peter laughed. "Next time we have PE, pick me first and you'll find out."

"You've got it, Parker," Flash said. He and Peter walked toward the exit, where Aunt May was waiting for them with their projects. "Hey, why don't we meet at the courts this weekend and practice some one-on-one?"

Peter smiled. He'd learned a lot today, and not just about ants. "You're on," he said.